⟨ **W9-AKD-102**

PAPL
DISCARDE

THE BEE AND THE DREAM

A

J A P A N E S E

T A L E

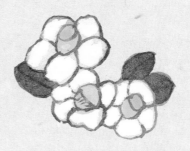

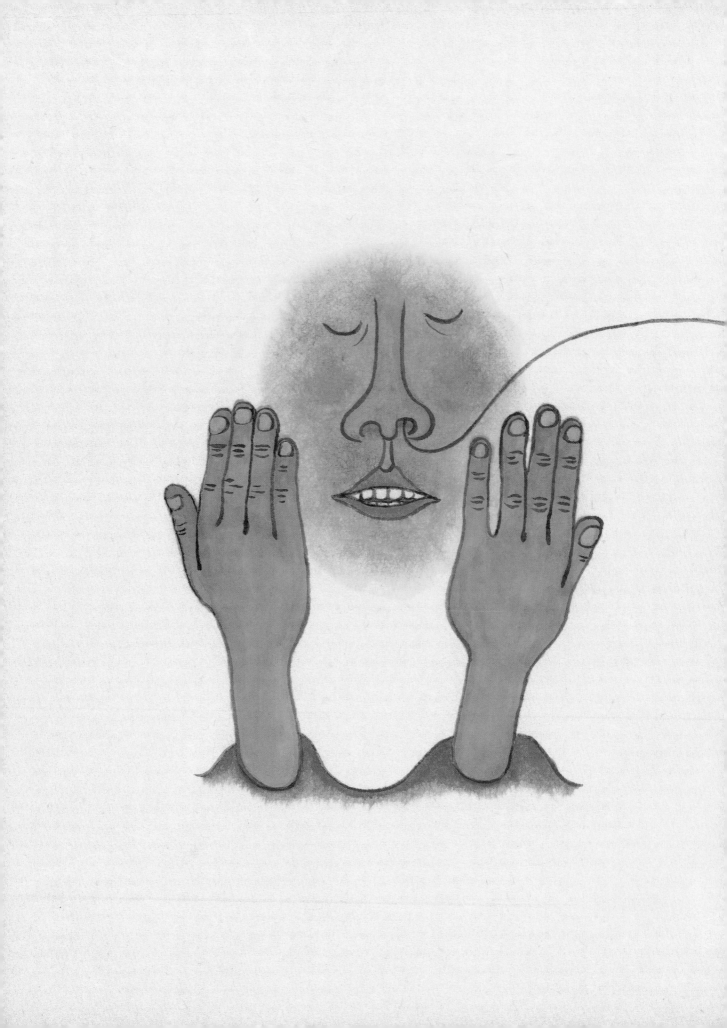

wapiti regional library

THE BEE
AND THE
DREAM

A JAPANESE TALE

adapted by JAN FREEMAN LONG

illustrated by KAORU ONO

DUTTON CHILDREN'S BOOKS | NEW YORK

With deepest appreciation to Margaret Scariano and Robert San Souci
J. F. L.

SOURCE NOTE

Researching this Japanese folktale, I found thirteen versions, all translated into English. I relied primarily on four of them, because their voices and detail offered me steady inspiration in adapting the tale to fit the picture-book format. From one oral transcription, "The Man Who Bought a Dream," in Richard Dorson's Folktales Told Around the World, *I borrowed five ideophones. I'm indebted to the University of Chicago Press for granting me permission to use them. I am also indebted to Junko Yokota for her careful reading of the text and her good suggestions.*

The publisher would like to thank Mariko Ogawa of Fukuinkan Shoten Publishers, Inc., for her kind offices in bringing this book to fruition.

Text copyright © 1996 by Jan Freeman Long ⎮ Illustrations copyright © 1996 by Kaoru Ono
All rights reserved. Published in the United States 1996 by Dutton Children's Books,
a division of Penguin Books USA Inc., 375 Hudson Street, New York, New York 10014
Designed by Sara Reynolds ⎮ Printed in Hong Kong ⎮ First Edition   10 9 8 7 6 5 4 3 2 1

LIBRARY OF CONGRESS CATALOGING-IN-PUBLICATION DATA
Long, Jan Freeman. The bee and the dream: a Japanese tale/adapted by Jan Freeman Long;
illustrated by Kaoru Ono.—1st ed.   p. cm.
Summary: Shin buys his friend Tasuke's dream from him and goes in search of the predicted fortune, only to be disappointed until, upon returning home, he receives a wonderful surprise.
ISBN 0-525-45287-7   [1. Folklore—Japan.]   I. Ono, Kaoru, date. ill.   II. Title.
PZ8.1.L943Be   1996   398.2'0952'02—dc20   94-43784   CIP   AC

The artwork for this book was done in Chinese ink and special paints used in Japanese-style painting known as *iwa-enogu*; the artist used a Japanese paper similar to mulberry paper.

In Japan there is an old saying:

WHEN YOU SEE A BEE FLY
FROM SOMEONE'S NOSE,
GOOD FORTUNE WILL BE YOURS.

Shin lived with his wife, Yuki, in a tiny village at the foot of a tall mountain. And, as any villager could tell you, they were hardworking peasants, respected by all.

Early every morning Shin and his friend Tasuke climbed up the mountain to gather cedar branches for firewood. At noon they shared a simple meal, and before sundown they sold their bundles of sticks at the marketplace.

One morning Shin glanced up at the sun. "I know it is early," he said, "but already I've worked hard and I'm tired."

"Let's have our meal now and take a little nap," said Tasuke.

So the two friends shared an *obento* of rice balls filled with pickled plum and fish. Then they lay down.

Tasuke fell right to sleep and was soon snoring loudly, *goo goo goo goo goo*. But Shin twisted and tossed and turned. "If I was tired before," he muttered, "why am I restless now?" Yet, no matter what he did, sleep would not come. So he contented himself with watching Tasuke's chest rise and fall and listening to the *goo goo goo* of his friend's snores.

After a while, the sleeping Tasuke rolled over and sighed, *uhhhhhnnnnnnn*. As he did so, a bee flew from his nose.

How odd! thought Shin. How did a bee get in my friend's nose?

Shortly after that, Tasuke woke up. "Did you have a good nap?" he asked Shin.

"I had no nap," Shin replied. "As soon as we lay down, I was wide awake. But listen to this. While you were sleeping, I saw a bee fly from your nose. Isn't that strange?"

"That is strange," said Tasuke, "especially since I myself felt nothing. I did have a dream, though—about a garden that belonged to the richest man in Naniwa! On top of a little hill was a tall pine tree, and next to the pine a white camellia bush bloomed. I don't know why, but I dug under the bush and found a jar filled with gold!"

"What a wonderful dream!" exclaimed Shin. "I'm sure you are meant to go to Naniwa! Did you find out the man's name?"

"He didn't tell me, and I forgot to ask," Tasuke teased.

"But you will go to Naniwa and look?" urged Shin.

Tasuke shrugged. "It was merely a midday dream, nothing more."

"But perhaps a fortune is waiting for you!" said Shin.

Tasuke frowned. "Let us speak no more of this nonsense."

Nevertheless, for the rest of the afternoon, Shin found one way or another to mention Naniwa to his friend. Finally, when the last of the firewood had been sold, Tasuke said, "Shin, if you believe so much in my dream, you may have it."

Shin was astounded. How could he take Tasuke's dream? Shouldn't he do something for it first, to make it his own?

"Tasuke," he said at last, "what if I pay you for it? I will buy your dream."

Tasuke shook his head over his friend's foolishness. Still, he accepted the few coins Shin placed in his hand.

"When I return with the gold, I will pay you much more," Shin promised.

That night Shin told his wife, Yuki, about the dream.

"You bought a dream!" she cried. "What nonsense! A dream can mean nothing if it isn't your own. Besides, we have no money to pay for a journey to Naniwa."

"Perhaps we could borrow enough from our relatives," Shin
replied. "When I return with the gold, I will pay everyone back."

Though Yuki protested, Shin finally persuaded her to help him.
A few days later, with a small purse tied to his waist, he set off.

Each day Shin walked as far as he could. The journey was long and difficult. Once, a violent rainstorm left him soaked and shivering. Later, a bear chased him. A few days after that, he narrowly escaped a band of thieves.

At last, Shin arrived in Naniwa. Weary yet excited, he asked people in the marketplace where the richest man in their city lived. A young boy led Shin to a splendid house.

"This is the home of Taro," said the boy, "the richest man in our city." Shin gave the boy a coin for his trouble and knocked on the door. When a servant answered, Shin asked to speak with the master of the house.

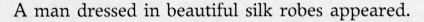

A man dressed in beautiful silk robes appeared.

"It is an honor to meet you, Taro-san," said Shin. "Forgive me for disturbing you. I am Shin, and I have walked for many days to find a certain garden."

"What does this have to do with me?" said the rich man.

"May I ask," began Shin, "is there a little hill in your garden?"

"There is...."

"And does a pine tree grow on top of the hill?"

"It does...."

"And next to the pine is a white camellia bush blooming?"

"What business of yours is my garden?" the rich man demanded. "How do you know what is there?"

"I know of a dream about a jar of gold buried under a camellia bush. If you permit me to dig in your garden, I will share the gold with you."

Now, the idea of gold greatly interested Taro. He glanced at the evening sky. "You must be hungry and tired. Come, be my guest tonight, and tomorrow you may dig under the camellia bush."

A servant led Shin to a pleasant room where he ate a warm meal and fell quickly to sleep.

Taro, however, remained wide awake, tossing and turning. "Who is this ragged stranger who thinks he can walk into my garden and dig up a jar of gold just like that?" Taro got up and instructed his servants to bring a shovel and lantern out to the garden.

"Dig here," he commanded, pointing beneath the camellia bush. The servants took turns. Little by little, the hole grew deeper. And then, *kotsun kotsun kotsun kotsun kotsun,* the shovel clinked against something solid.

"That must be it!" cried Taro. "Lift it out, lift it out, hurry up!"

As his servants struggled with the heavy jar, Taro reached down and pulled off the lid. *Ba jaba jaba jaba ja boon boon boon!* With a thunderous noise, something like a swarm of angry bees flew out of the jar and disappeared.

When all was quiet, Taro peered inside. Nothing but darkness. He stuck his arm in and felt all around. Only damp air. Once more he looked inside. Truly, the jar was empty.

With an angry wave he ordered, "Put it back in the ground and make everything look as before." Then he returned to his house.

The next morning Taro led Shin to the garden. "We planted this camellia bush a few days ago and saw no gold. But you are welcome to dig."

Shin took the shovel. Soon he would give Taro a share of the gold, and then he would carry the rest home to repay everyone.

Indeed, in a few moments, *kotsun kotsun kotsun kotsun kotsun,* the shovel clinked against something solid. Shin could hardly contain his excitement. He reached into the hole, pulled out the jar, raised the lid, and...

Inside he saw nothing.

He shook the jar back and forth, back and forth. Only silence. He reached in. Only damp air.

Shin was stricken. How could the jar be empty? Had the dream meant nothing after all? He felt weak with shame. "I've made a terrible mistake," he said. "I thought the jar would be full of gold, and I would share it with you. But instead I've dug a hole in your garden for nothing. Please, take the rest of my coins and forgive me for the trouble I've caused."

In despair, Shin left the rich man's house. He went on his way without food or safe lodging. He begged from strangers. "It is true," he cried, "I am a fool. I spent borrowed money, and I have nothing to show for it. I am nothing now but a disgrace to my family. It would be better if I never went home." And when Shin came to a road that led away from his village, he took it.

But as he walked, new thoughts came to him. "My wife and my relatives deserve to know what has happened. And I must try to repay them for their generosity."

So Shin turned again toward home.

Many days later, he arrived at his own little village. When his wife saw him, she ran out to meet him.

"My dear husband," she called. "Come quickly! I've been waiting and waiting for you. Something amazing happened while you were gone."

"Now what misfortune has befallen us?" Shin murmured.

"Many nights ago, something like a swarm of angry bees flew into our house," Yuki explained. "The noise, *gara gara gara gara gara,* was like thunder. I thought the walls would crumble. I ran outside and hid under a tree.

"When it was quiet, I crept back inside. You can't imagine what I found!"

Shin followed his wife into their home. What he saw filled him with wonder.

Gold coins, precious silks, coral, jade, and other treasures glistened and sparkled, *pika pika pika pika pika,* everywhere.

"It's true," Yuki rejoiced. "I left everything exactly where it fell so you could see for yourself."

The next day Shin repaid his relatives many times over. He gave an especially large bag of gold and jewels to Tasuke. "For your dream," he said.

Shin and Yuki lived well the rest of their days, respected by all. As for Tasuke, from then on he gladly told Shin every dream that came to him.

So it is:

IF GOOD FORTUNE

IS MEANT FOR YOU,

NO MATTER WHAT HAPPENS,

IT WILL BE YOURS.

j 398.209 LON
Long, Jan Freeman.
The bee and the dream : a
33292006408730   PA

APR 27 2009